# CONCRETE MIXERS

by Katie Chanez

**Cody Koala**
An Imprint of Pop!
popbooksonline.com

abdobooks.com
Published by Pop!, a division of ABDO, PO Box 398166, Minneapolis, Minnesota 55439. Copyright © 2020 by POP, LLC. International copyrights reserved in all countries. No part of this book may be reproduced in any form without written permission from the publisher. Pop!™ is a trademark and logo of POP, LLC.

Printed in the United States of America, North Mankato, Minnesota
052019
092019

**THIS BOOK CONTAINS RECYCLED MATERIALS**

Cover Photo: iStockphoto
Interior Photos: iStockphoto, 1, 5 (top), 5 (bottom left), 5 (bottom right), 7, 11, 13, 14, 17, 19, 20, 21; Shutterstock Images, 8
Editor: Meg Gaertner
Series Designer: Jake Slavik

Library of Congress Control Number: 2018964592
Publisher's Cataloging-in-Publication Data
Names: Chanez, Katie, author.
Title: Concrete mixers / by Katie Chanez.
Description: Minneapolis, Minnesota : Pop!, 2020 | Series: Construction vehicles | Includes online resources and index.
Identifiers: ISBN 9781532163296 (lib. bdg.) | ISBN 9781644940020 (pbk.) | ISBN 9781532164736 (ebook)
Subjects: LCSH: Concrete mixers--Juvenile literature. | Construction equipment--Juvenile literature. | Construction industry--Equipment and supplies--Juvenile literature.
Classification: DDC 629.225--dc23

## Hello! My name is
# Cody Koala

Pop open this book and you'll find QR codes like this one, loaded with information, so you can learn even more!

Scan this code* and others like it while you read, or visit the website below to make this book pop.

**popbooksonline.com/concrete-mixers**

*Scanning QR codes requires a web-enabled smart device with a QR code reader app and a camera.

# Table of Contents

**Chapter 1**
The Concrete
Mixer Can Help!. . . . . . . 4

**Chapter 2**
A Concrete Mixer's Job . . . 6

**Chapter 3**
Parts of a Concrete Mixer   12

**Chapter 4**
Types of Concrete Mixers .  18

Making Connections . . . . . . . . 22
Glossary. . . . . . . . . . . . . . . . 23
Index . . . . . . . . . . . . . . . . . 24
Online Resources . . . . . . . . . . 24

## Chapter 1

# The Concrete Mixer Can Help!

A **concrete** mixer pours out wet concrete. Workers smooth the concrete out. The concrete **sets**. It makes a hard road.

Watch a video here!

Chapter 2

# A Concrete Mixer's Job

**Concrete** mixers carry wet concrete. They bring the concrete to construction areas.

Learn more here!

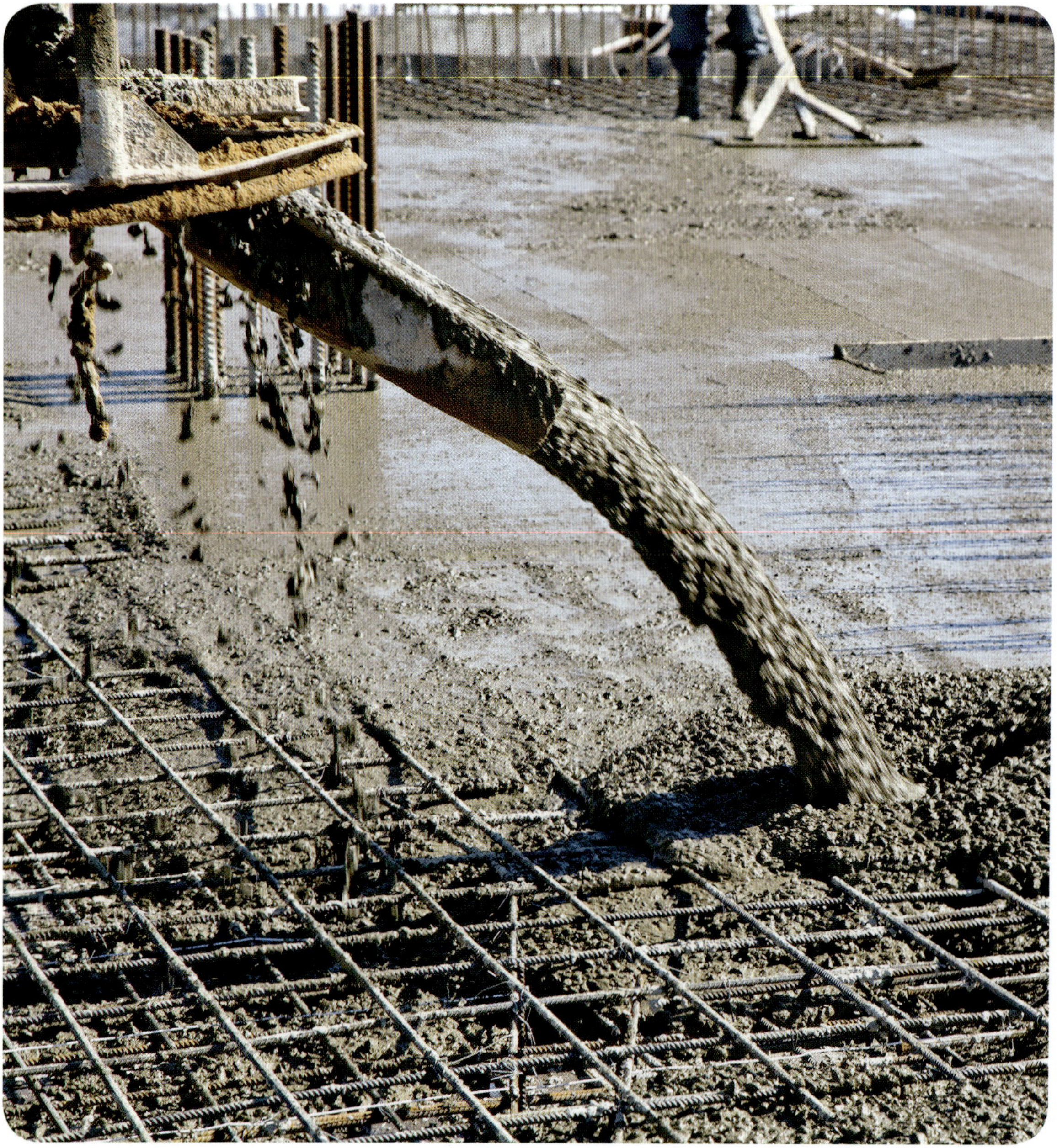

Concrete becomes very hard when it **sets**. Workers do not want it to set too soon.

> Concrete is used to make roads, bridges, and tall buildings.

Concrete mixers stir the concrete. They keep it from setting. Workers pour the wet concrete in the right area. The concrete hardens there.

> People have been using concrete for thousands of years.

11

### Chapter 3

# Parts of a Concrete Mixer

A **concrete** mixer is a kind of truck. It moves on wheels. The truck has a powerful **engine**. It provides power to move the heavy concrete.

> A concrete mixer can drive through a solid wall!

Complete an activity here!

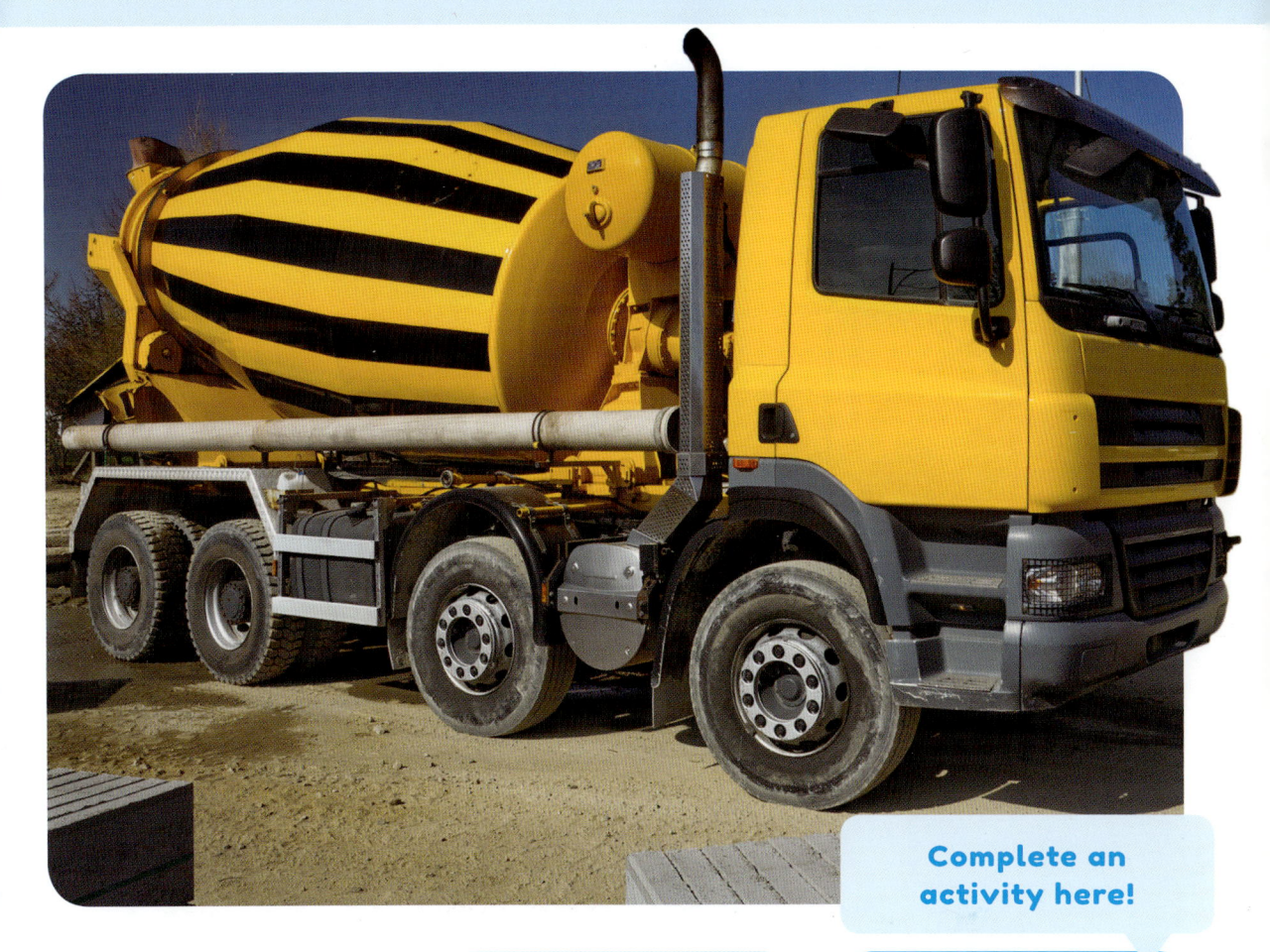

13

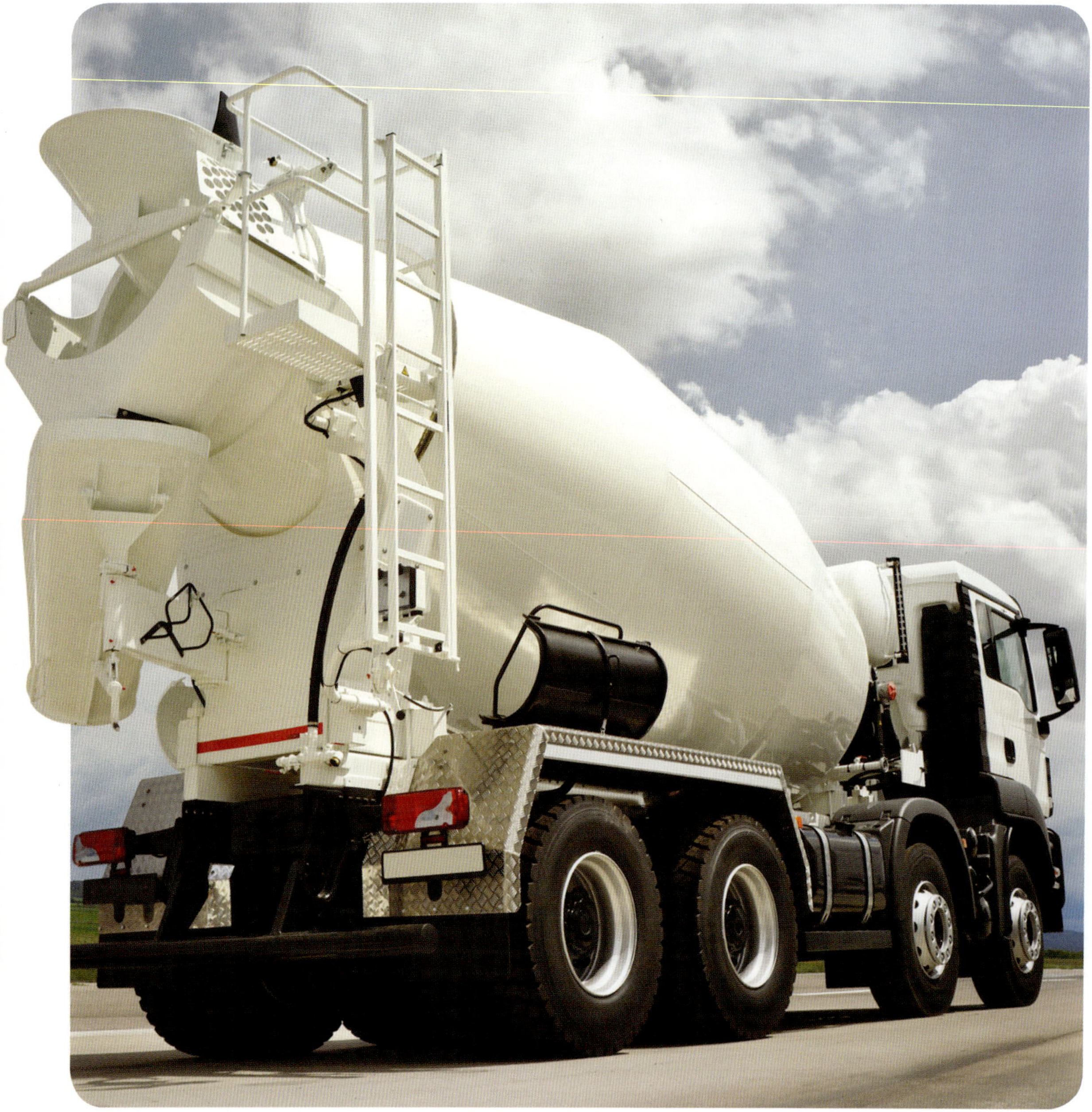

The **drum** holds the wet concrete. The drum spins constantly. It stirs the concrete. It mixes the concrete and keeps it from **setting**.

At the back of the drum is a **chute**. Wet concrete flows down the chute. Workers use the chute to place the concrete.

> The first concrete mixers were pulled by horses.

drum

truck

chute

Chapter 4

# Types of Concrete Mixers

Some **concrete** mixers have a **chute** in front. These mixers are often easier for workers to use. The driver can control where the concrete goes from inside the truck.

chute

Learn more here!

19

Some concrete mixers are filled away from the construction area. They drive to the construction area.

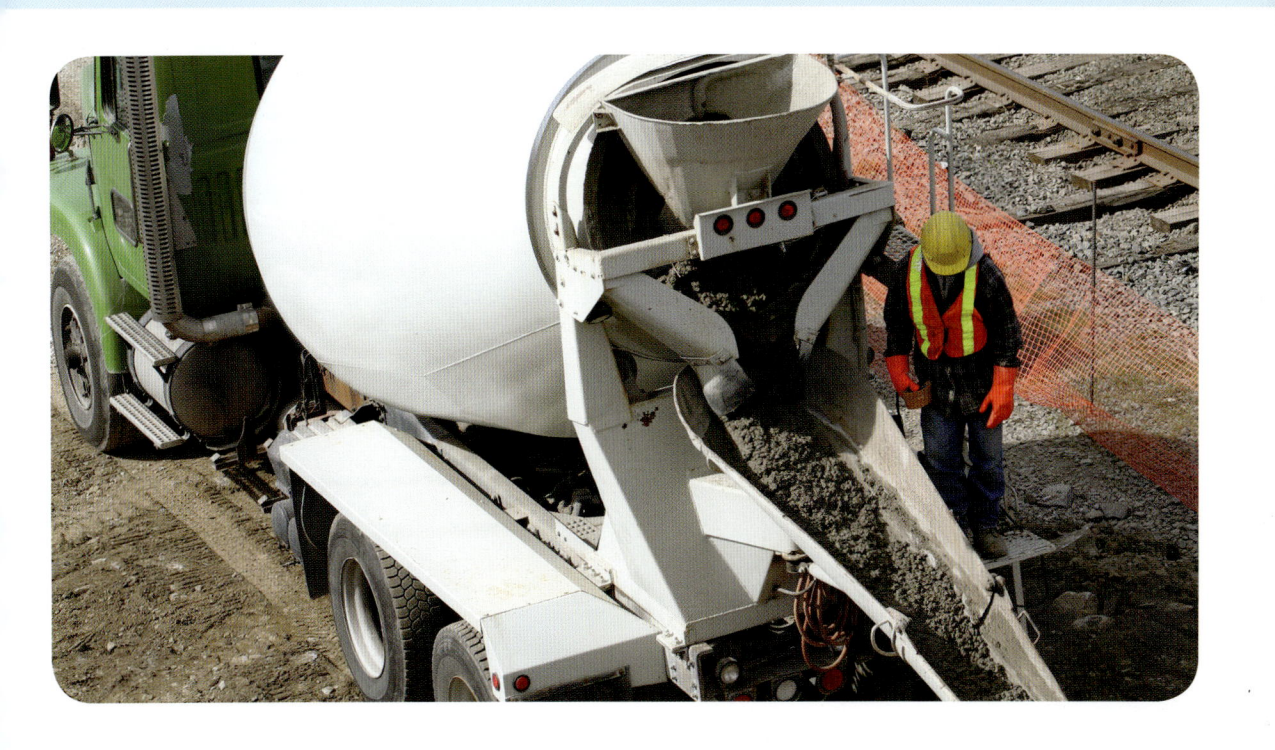

They bring the concrete with them. Others have concrete made inside them right on the spot.

# Making Connections

## Text-to-Self

Have you ever seen a concrete mixer? Where did you see it? What was it doing?

## Text-to-Text

Have you read about another construction truck? How is it similar to a concrete mixer? How is it different?

## Text-to-World

People use concrete to build many things. What other materials do people use for building?

# Glossary

**chute** – a slide used to move things from a higher place to a lower place.

**concrete** – a strong material used to build roads, bridges, and buildings.

**drum** – the back part of a concrete mixer where wet concrete is stored and mixed.

**engine** – a machine that makes things move.

**set** – to become very hard after drying.

# Index

chutes, 16, 17, 18

drums, 15, 16, 17

engines, 12

roads, 4, 9

stirring, 10, 15

wheels, 12

## Online Resources

## popbooksonline.com

Thanks for reading this Cody Koala book!

Scan this code* and others like it in this book, or visit the website below to make this book pop!

popbooksonline.com/concrete-mixers

*Scanning QR codes requires a web-enabled smart device with a QR code reader app and a camera.